About the Author

Inspiration for this story came from engaging walks along Norfolk and Suffolk's coastal beach hut spots. Whilst enjoying the variety of styles, names and colours of beach huts, the author realised that they had characters and personalities of their own, and stories and adventures they could share.

The Lonely Beach Hut

Andy Kemp

Illustrations by Amy Smith

The Lonely Beach Hut

Olympia Publishers
London

www.olympiapublishers.com
OLYMPIA PAPERBACK EDITION

A CIP catalogue record for this title is
available from the British Library.

ISBN: 978-1-78830-467-2

This is a work of fiction.
Names, characters, places and incidents originate from the writer's
imagination. Any resemblance to actual persons, living or dead, is
purely coincidental.

First Published in 2020
Tallis House
2 Tallis Street
London
EC4Y 0AB
Printed in Great Britain

Dedication

For all beach huts, and their adventures - everywhere

Acknowledgements

With thanks to my family for support. To Sian Osborne for graphic interpretation and to Amy Smith, for understanding how the illustrations in my head could appear on paper.

Far away at the end of a long promenade
stood a beach hut.
It was a rather dilapidated beach hut.
It had been forgotten for a long time
and the beach hut was lonely.

He sat alone at this end of the beach,
away from all the families and the cafes.

He was toppling forward being old and in
need of repair, but he could see there were
children with kites, dogs with balls,
deckchairs and drinks.

It all looked so colourful and fun!

The wind carried the noises and he
could hear laughter and squeals,
and knew these were happy times
at that end of the beach.

The lonely beach hut looked around him.
There wasn't any golden sand, buckets and spades and fun times.

No happy noises or people.
There was only the dunes and weedy plants with shingle around him. Bits of sea flotsam – driftwood, old ropes and bottles were left beside him.

The lonely beach hut felt sad. Sometimes he thought a dog walker, or a family would come towards him. He hoped they might say hello, perhaps give his tired old wood a rub better. But no-one came.
Even the excitable dogs off a lead would still run past him, preferring to cock their leg on the spikey grass rather than on him.

The lonely beach hut thought this would always be so.
He would get even older. Fall more to bits until he imagined
he would just disintegrate and blend into the shingle and be
lost as driftwood.

But what was this?
One day, the lonely beach hut could see a different activity
at the far end of the beach. As well as the families, there
were bright upright things being put up on the promenade.

What were these buildings?
More cafes? Shops? Toilets? Kennels?
The lonely beach hut strained forward and squinted his eyes in the sunshine trying to get a better look. There seemed to be more people of all ages with children of all ages, and dogs of all sizes and shapes.
What was going on??

Day by day, there were more of these little houses (the lonely beach hut decided they were little houses as he could see people bringing all sorts of comforts into them).
Some little houses had carpets, kitchens, stoves, very comfortable looking chairs and were very smartly decorated, not at all like the beach type shed he originally was.
And these little houses were being erected along the promenade. They were getting closer to the lonely beach hut.

As the little houses got nearer to the lonely beach hut,
it also brought people and their things with children and
dogs closer to him.
It was all very interesting to observe, and almost
exciting, except it made the lonely beach hut have pangs of
envy.
He wished he could look that smart and have a family
furnish him with their fashionable things.

But who was going to bother with him, stuck up the wrong end of the long path, far from the golden sands and cafes? He had to accept he was always going to be a lonely beach hut and grow old and alone.

And as tears welled in his eyes, he didn't see the people coming his way. Not until they were beside him, did he hear them say, "This will do. It will be great."
What was this? What did they mean? And then he saw two people, a middle-aged couple smiling at him.

And the next day, they came again. This time with
two younger (but grown up) people. What were they
doing?They were repairing him! He was being painted!
Oh, HOW WONDERFUL!
The lonely beach hut could feel himself straightening up
and feeling re-energised with his new look painted finish.
How smart he must be.

Maybe not as grand as the little houses (he now learned
from the kind people 'doing him up' that they were beach huts
- like him!) They were new and bigger.
But he felt respectable and proud of
being a traditional beach hut.

Very soon the new big beach huts were almost to the end of the promenade path and near to him. Would they mind being close to him, who is smaller and older?
The lonely beach hut felt rather anxious. Would the new beach huts talk to him? Would they be haughty and ignore him? Oh dear, what could he do?
He looked nervously at them all, hoping they wouldn't make fun of him or be unkind.

"So," one said. "You must have seen so much; you must have so many stories you can tell us."
"Oh yes," said another. "We can't wait to hear your tales, you have so much more experience than us."
And there seemed to be a huge murmur of approval and recognition from all the new beach huts of the importance of him – this old beach hut soldier.

The lonely beach hut felt himself puff up with pride. He had value. He had knowledge. And, he realized, he had company. Maybe in time, he would also have friends.
The next day, feeling quite alive, the lonely beach hut looked down the promenade and was smiling at how busy the seaside was and enjoying the coming and goings at all the new beach huts.

Suddenly to his delight, he saw the couple who had restored
him, coming along the promenade with the younger couple too.
But who else was this coming with them?
It was another old soldier like him,
being a bit bent with his stick and cap who was helped along b
two very much smaller beings – children!
Oh, the lonely beach hut couldn't believe it. His little heart
nearly gave out it was beating so fast. What was missing?
Nothing.

Then the children called out 'Popsy' and bounding straight to the picnic basket came — a dog!
This dear old man, two children and a dog, a young couple and an older couple were opening up the lonely beach hut doors, patting him and thanking him for being such a trusty strong old beach hut.

They were, they told him, his new family.
His family.
His own beach hut family.
It was so wonderful; the lonely beach hut
could grin and flap his doors in delight. And
as the lonely beach hut looked around, he
knew he wouldn't be lonely now, as he wasn't
on his own anymore.

Can you find the seagull hidden on all the pages?

Colour and name your own Beach Hut.

GLOSSARY

ANXIOUS: Feeling worried

COCK A LEG: dogs lifting a back leg to do a wee

DILAPIDATED: Falling to bits

DISINTEGRATE: Completely fall to bits and disappear

DUNES: Tough spikey grass growing on beach

ERECTED: Being made and put up

EXPERIENCE: Things you have done and know about

FASHIONABLE: new 'must haves'

FLOTSAM: Rubbish the sea didn't want

HAUGHTY: Thinking you are better than someone else

IGNORE: Not noticing on purpose

OBSERVE: Look at

PROMENADE: Long wide walkway

RECOGNITION: Knowing who or what something is

REPAIR: Making something work or become whole again

RE-ENERGISED: Feeling full of energy

RESPECTABLE: That you are ok

RESTORED: Made good again

SHINGLE: Masses of small stones on the beach

TRADITIONAL: Always been like that